EDUARDO GUADARDO, ELITE SHEEP

by Anthony Pearson
Illustrated by Jennifer E. Morris

two lions

For Cora
—A. P.

For Scott
—J. E. M.

Published by Two Lions, New York

www.apub.com

Amazon, the Amazon logo, and Two Lions are
trademarks of Amazon.com, Inc., or its affiliates.

ISBN-13: 9781503902909

ISBN-10: 1503902900

The illustrations are rendered in digital media

Book design by Tanya Ross-Hughes

Printed in China

First Edition

10 9 8 7 6 5 4 3 2 1

Hello. I'm Eduardo Guadardo.
I'm about to graduate from the FBI.

That's the Fairy-Tale Bureau of Investigations
in case you were wondering.

I look fluffy. I look cute.
But I'm no little lamb.

I'm going to be an **Elite Sheep.**

SQUIRREL CAM 07

REC O 2:25:03:01

I know **five** forms of kung fu.

I can **outfox** the foxiest foxes.

I can **outsniff** the sniffiest dogs.

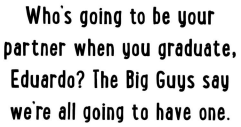

And these perpetrators (that we agents call "bad guys")—Wolf, Troll, and Witch—have teamed up to catch her. They think the farmer will pay them a zillion dollars to get her back.

I'm going to keep Mary safe. No matter what.

WANTED

Name: Witch
Skin: Green
Hair: Witchy
Alert: Very dangerous

968525

Name: Wolf
Fur: Gray
Teeth: Sharp

652981

Name: Troll
Resides: Under bridge
Associates: Wolf and Witch

825876

This is definitely a job for someone **baaaaaaad**.
Like me. Eduardo Guadardo, soon-to-be **Elite Sheep**.

So I go incognito. (That's undercover. ya know.)

That's when Mary and I meet for the first time.
She falls for my super adorable sheep style.

OOOOOOOhhhh! You are the cutest little lamb!
Your fleece is white as snow! I think I'll love you and
keep you and play with you FOREVER and EVER and EVER.
You can follow me wherever I go.

What a sweet kid.
This should be easy.

And it was easy. Sort of.
See, Mary can be a bit adventurous.

WHEEEEEEEEEEEEEEEEEEE!

SKILL SUMMARY FOR:

Eduardo Guadardo

	Superb
SPEED	Superb
SMARTS	Superb
SKILLS	Totally Terrible
TEAMWORK	

Championship Rowing Regatta

Suggested partner???

QUIZ BOWL

Sheep Wins Kung Fu Competition

To be honest, I felt a bit sheepish.
And not the elite kind.
I had some work to do.

And you know what?
The whole teamwork thing went pretty well.
We were able to pull for one another.

It didn't take a genius to see that it made
all of us stronger, faster, and smarter. Even me.

So it's official. I'm now Junior Agent Eduardo Guadardo, **Elite Sheep**. My partner? Special Agent Mary Sawyer, Expert in Disguise and Subterfuge (that means pulling the wool over your eyes).

It turns out Little Bo Peep has lost her sheep, and
Mary and I have to find them. And we're going to.
You know why?
Because we're one **baaaaaaaaaaaaaad** team.
You know, the elite kind.

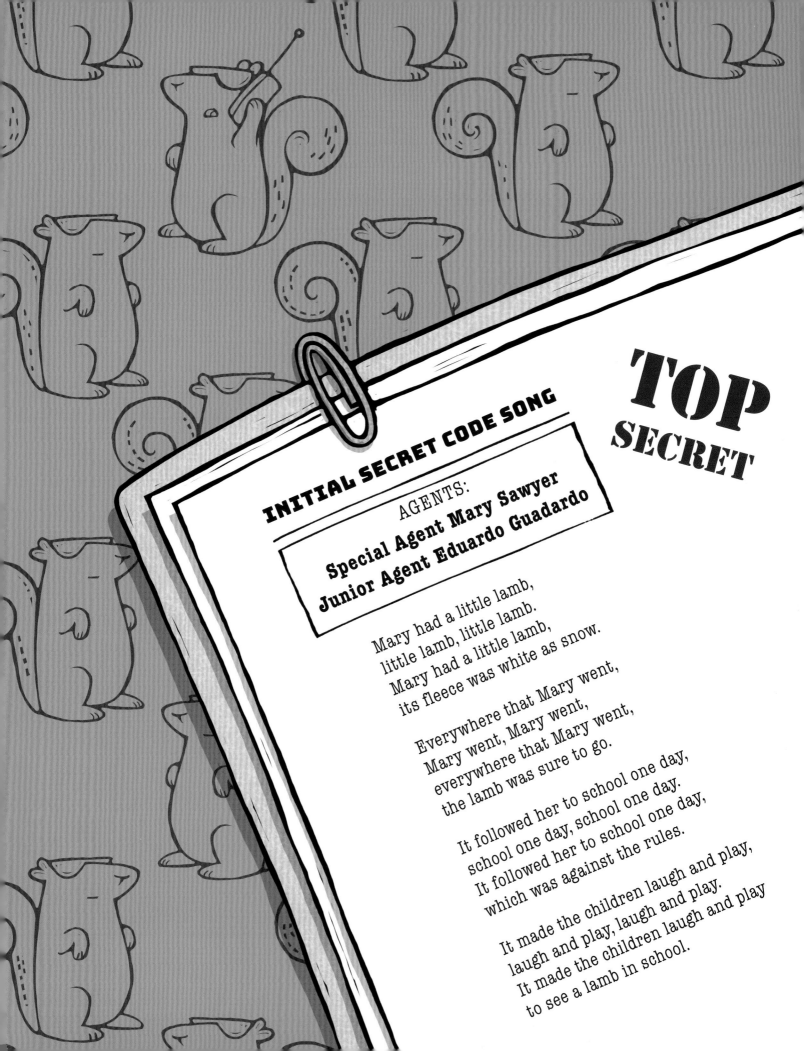

INITIAL SECRET CODE SONG

AGENTS:
Special Agent Mary Sawyer
Junior Agent Eduardo Guadardo

Mary had a little lamb,
little lamb, little lamb.
Mary had a little lamb,
its fleece was white as snow.

Everywhere that Mary went,
Mary went, Mary went,
everywhere that Mary went,
the lamb was sure to go.

It followed her to school one day,
school one day, school one day.
It followed her to school one day,
which was against the rules.

It made the children laugh and play,
laugh and play, laugh and play.
It made the children laugh and play
to see a lamb in school.